This edition published by Parragon Books Ltd in 2015 and distributed by

Parragon Inc.
440 Park Avenue South, 13th Floor
New York, NY 10016
www.parragon.com

ISBN 978-1-4748-3133-8

Printed in China

Chicken Little

Retold by Ronne Randall

Illustrated by Nicola Evans

PaRragon

Bath • New York • Cologne • Melbourne • Delhi
Hong Kong • Shenzhen • Singapore • Amsterdam

One day, Chicken Little was walking down the road, thinking his own thoughts about everything and nothing, when . . .

THWACK!

An acorn fell on his head!

"Ouch!" said Chicken Little, rubbing his head.
"I think the sky is falling! I must run and tell the king!"

So Chicken Little ran down the road to tell the king. And on his way he met Henny Penny.

"Where are you going in such a hurry?"

Henny Penny asked Chicken Little.

"The sky is falling, and I am going to tell the king!" said Chicken Little.

"I will come with you," said Henny Penny.

So Henny Penny and Chicken Little rushed down the road to tell the king. And on their way they met Cocky Locky.

"Where are you going in such a hurry?"

Cocky Locky asked them.

"The sky is falling, and we are going to tell the king!" said Chicken Little.

"I will come with you," said Cocky Locky.

So Cocky Locky, Henny Penny, and Chicken Little dashed down the road to tell the king. And on their way they met Ducky Lucky.

"Where are you going in such a hurry?"

Ducky Lucky asked them.

"The sky is falling, and we are going to tell the king," said Chicken Little.

"I will come with you," said Ducky Lucky.

So Ducky Lucky,

Cocky Locky,

Henny Penny,

and Chicken Little

scurried down the road to tell the king. And on their way
they met Drakey Lakey.

"Where are you going in such a hurry?"

Drakey Lakey asked.

"The sky is falling, and we are going to tell the king," said Chicken Little.

I will come with you," said Drakey Lakey.

So Drakey Lakey, Ducky Lucky, Cocky Locky, Henny Penny, and Chicken Little scampered down the road to tell the king. And on their way they met Goosey Loosey.

"Where are you going in such a hurry?" asked Goosey Loosey.

"The sky is falling, and we are going to tell the king," said Chicken Little.

"I will come with you," said Goosey Loosey.

So Goosey Loosey, Drakey Lakey, Ducky Lucky, Cocky Locky, Henny Penny, and Chicken Little hurried down the road to tell the king. And on their way they met Turkey Lurkey.

"Where are you going in such a hurry?"

asked Turkey Lurkey.

"The sky is falling, and we are going to tell the king," said Chicken Little.

"I will come with you," said Turkey Lurkey.

So Turkey Lurkey, Goosey Loosey, Drakey Lakey, Ducky Lucky, Cocky Locky, Henny Penny, and Chicken Little raced down the road to tell the king. And on their way they met Foxy Loxy.

"Why, good day, my friends!"
said Foxy Loxy.
"And where
might you all be
going on this fine
morning?"

"The sky is falling," said Chicken Little.
"We are going to tell the king!"

"Really?

How interesting. Have you ever been to the king's palace before?" asked Foxy Loxy.

"No," said Chicken Little. The others all shook their heads.

"Then how do you know you will find the way?" asked Foxy Loxy.

"Um . . . I never thought of that," said Chicken Little.

"Why don't you let me help you?" said Foxy Loxy.

"I know the way to the king's palace very well. Just follow me, and you will be there in no time!"

So Chicken Little, Henny Penny, Cocky
Locky, Ducky Lucky, Drakey Lakey, Goosey
Loosey, and Turkey Lurkey all followed
Foxy Loxy down the road.

Soon they came to a path that led into the woods.

They followed Foxy Loxy down the path . . .

into the woods . . .

and straight to Foxy Loxy's den!

Foxy Loxy's wife and babies were waiting there, all ready to gobble up Chicken Little, Henny Penny, Cocky Locky, Ducky Lucky, Drakey Lakey, Goosey Loosey, and Turkey Lurkey!

So Turkey Lurkey, Goosey Loosey, Drakey Lakey, Ducky Lucky, Cocky Locky, Henny Penny, and Chicken Little all **ran** and **flapped** and **flew** away as fast as they could!

And they never did
get to tell the king that
the sky was falling.

The End